PRESTO AND ZESTO IN LIMBOLAND

PRESTO and ZESTO in LIMBOLAND

STORY BY
ARTHUR YORINKS
AND **MAURICE SENDAK**

PICTURES BY
MAURICE SENDAK

AFTERWORD BY ARTHUR YORINKS

MICHAEL DI CAPUA BOOKS · HARPERCOLLINS PUBLISHERS

Library of Congress control number: 2017963819

HarperCollins Publishers, New York, NY 10007

Original art digitally scanned by Stinehour Editions

Designed by Steve Scott

Printed and bound by Phoenix Color

First edition, 2018

18 19 20 21 22   PC   10 9 8 7 6 5 4 3 2 1

IT WAS THURSDAY—no, no, it was Saturday when—no, wait a minute. I think it was Sunday—oh, I don't remember what day it was, but one day Presto and Zesto, good friends, took a walk and ended up in Limboland.

They didn't mean to go there, who would go there, but they had a lot on their minds, and to tell you the truth they were both upset that there wasn't any cake for lunch.

"Have you noticed," they talked as they walked, "that you just can't get good cake anymore, and what's the world coming to without cake?"

Before they knew it, they took a turn and . . .

"Uh-oh," said Presto.

"We're in Limboland!" said Zesto.

Yikes.

They were in Limboland all right, for along came a maniac shepherd boy with two animals, goats, I think. Presto and Zesto froze.

"There's not much time before the wedding!" the boy said with his eyes popping out. They were popping out because his pants were too tight.

"Wedding?" Presto asked. "What wedding?"

"*What wedding?*" the boy shouted. "The sugar beets! The sugar beets are getting married! And you better find a present!"

Presto and Zesto had seen maniacs before but never one with such a big stick, so Presto quickly said, "Oh, sure, the sugar beets wedding, of course, we're looking for a present right now."

"By the way," asked Zesto, "will there be cake?"

The boy went zonkers, being that he was The Boy Who Only Eats Cake.

"YES!" he said. "Cake, cake, cake, cake, cake, cake, CAKE!"

"Well, at least there'll be cake," said Presto to Zesto. They took two steps and—lo and behold—another goat. An old goat.

"Excuse me," called Presto. "We're looking for a present—"

"Aren't we all," grumbled the goat. "The whole town is looking for a present for the happy couple. But there's only one, and Bumbo's got it."

"Bumbo?" asked Zesto.

"Bumbo, the monster. He has a set of bagpipes, the perfect present, but he'll set fire to the town before he gives *them* up."

"Oh," sighed Presto.

"And don't think of going near him. He'll tear your pants off and feed you to his pet spider."

"*Oh!*" said Zesto.

"But, then again," said the goat, "if nobody brings a present, there won't be a wedding, and if there's no wedding, we'll all be stuck in Limboland forever."

"OH!" cried Presto *and* Zesto.

Not wanting to be stuck in Limboland forever, what a thought, Presto and Zesto decided to find Bumbo and get his bagpipes.

"Has anyone seen Bumbo?" they shouted in the town square. "Anyone?"

The mayor shivered. "B-B-Bumbo?" he said. "Oh, boys, d-don't go near *him*!"

The baker, who kept all her animals on her front porch, yelled out, "Don't you mention that monster! You're scaring my babies!"

Her prize bull did look upset. Like, really upset. Like, *"I'm going to bite you!"* upset. So Presto and Zesto tippy-toed away and soon came upon a family thoroughly enjoying the fresh air.

"Hello," said Presto. "We're looking for Bumbo and—" The second the name Bumbo was heard, a boy who had strayed from his marching band covered his ears and a couple of goats—everybody has goats in Limboland—went berserk.

"Whoa!" said the wood chopper, who was slicing bread. "If I see this Bumbo, I do GREAT damage to his whole entire body! Wham, *bam*, SLAM!" His wife nodded.

"But," he continued, "who knows where Bumbo is? I don't know." The chopper lifted his chopper. "You guys hungry?"

One look at the size of it—the chopper's chopper—and Presto and Zesto thought it best to push on.

Around the bend, a bear was busy getting his wedding outfit ready. Zesto sidled up and asked, "Have you seen Bumbo?"

Instantly, the bear's friend, who had been eating Limboland porridge (it's made from—oh, you don't want to know what it's made from), leapt into the air and cried, "*I* want to see Bumbo!"

"*Now look!*" growled the bear. "Junior was sitting and eating so nicely and you had to bring up . . . You Know Who!"

The bear had scissors and Zesto remembered what his mother always said: "If you see a bear with scissors—RUN!"

And so they did. They ran.

Down the road a smidge, Presto and Zesto stopped to listen to the wedding band. They were rehearsing a boffo duet:

You have to be a dimbo, to live in Limbo,
Woe is me, I've been in Limbo all my life.
But we'll all get to leave this land of Limbo
When the sugar beets are husband and wife!

Oh please find Bumbo, that gumbo-eating dumbo,
Mister Bumbo with bagpipes in hand.
Our thanks will be jumbo when you clobber that crum-bo
And we all say goodbye to Limboland!

Heartily inspired, Presto and Zesto zipped right along.

Deep in the woods, they caught the wedding caterer testing his new cooking pot.

"Hi there!" said Zesto, trying to be cheerful. "Do you know which way to Bumbo's house?"

"Bumbo!" shrieked the caterer's wife. "That crook! That thief! He still owes us five bubkes," which is a lot of money in Limboland, "and if I ever get my hands on him, I'll, I'll . . ." She ran away she was so verklempt.

"Mama," said her son, "can I play in the pot next? Please, Mama?"

Presto and Zesto slunk off. Would they ever find Bumbo? *Would they ever get out of Limboland?*

They walked and walked and walked and walked until finally they came upon an old woman from the old country, the country where only old people live. Naturally she knew some spells, and there she was, using mumbo-jumbo and heebie-jeebie, trying to put out a fire started by Bumbo.

Bumbo?

Bumbo! He must be close, he must live nearby! Presto and Zesto wished the old woman luck and sprinted out the door.

Ah, BUMBO! That mean-o! That stink-o! That beast! There he was, all ugly and hairy and smelly and scaly. He'd torn Presto's pants off and was just about to feed him to his spider when Zesto, on a willing horse, charged.

With a diddly-dee and a hippity-ho, Zesto grabbed Bumbo's bagpipes while his horse kicked him right in the knee.

"Hey! That hurt!" Bumbo yelled as Zesto picked up Presto, and away they rode, just in time for the wedding of the sugar beets.

What a lovely wedding it was, moonlight and all. The sugar beets adored their present, who wouldn't, and though Presto and Zesto were so hungry they could have eaten both the bride *and* the groom, there was CAKE!

Yes, the cake was delicious, as cakes tend to be in Limboland, and Presto and Zesto had two pieces each before they said their fond goodbyes and returned home, safe and sound.

Afterword

Some things are meant to be. So it is with this book. It might have been lost forever. Here's how it came to be in the first place and how it came to be found.

First, you should know that Maurice and I were friends for over forty years and, on occasion, collaborators. One of those collaborations was The Night Kitchen Theater, and it could be said that the pictures in this book were conceived at the same time as our nascent theater company.

In 1990, Maurice was asked to provide pictures to be used as projections for a London Symphony Orchestra performance of Janacek's *Rikadla*, a 1927 composition that sets a series of nursery rhymes for instruments and voices. These nonsense rhymes appeared originally in a popular Czech newspaper, accompanied by illustrations by Josef Lada.

So, while referencing the Lada originals, Maurice produced a suite of ten pictures illustrating the rhymes that are, well, pure Sendak. I vividly remember seeing them for the first time in all their glorious cuckoo-ness—brave, funny, brimming with color and intensity. What a shame that they would be seen just once.

It's true; Maurice did bring them out again—again as projections—for a 1997 concert benefitting the educational foundation Midori and Friends. But then, as Maurice would say, it was genug (enough). The pictures were put in a drawer and there they remained.

But I never forgot about them. Would you? I don't think so. About three years later, while Maurice and I were talking over lunch about work, I mentioned the Sugar Beets pictures (as we called them). They could be a book, no? We both agreed, yes. But what was the story?

We took the pictures out and arranged them on his drawing table. Right then and there, in his studio, like some manic vaudevillian team, we began riffing on a story that might turn these disparate pictures into a cohesive picture book.

In a fit of homage to our own friendship, we wove a tale

about two friends and named them after ourselves—Presto and Zesto—ridiculous nicknames we had given each other. Oh, how I wish this brainstorming session had been recorded, for all I specifically remember of that afternoon is being in Maurice's studio with both of us laughing like crazy. We were two short jazz musicians, two storytellers improvising off of each other.

On scraps of paper, I took some notes. Over the course of a few months—and yes, plenty of cake and many walks—we crafted a narrative. Using those notes (now lost), I typed out a complete draft and presented it to Maurice. He read it. He made suggestions. I made suggestions. We both declared it a picture book. Then . . . this happened, that happened. He went on to other things. So did I. Eventually, both of us forgot about the manuscript. In the interim, our pop-up book, *Mommy?*, rose to the fore. Time passed. And so did Maurice. He was gone.

The silence of a friendship lost was deafening. Then, out of nowhere, fifteen years after this (unpublished) picture book partnership, came a note from Lynn Caponera. Lynn, Maurice's friend, assistant, and everything person, had been going through some files and found an odd typescript with an equally odd title: *Presto and Zesto in Limboland*. She instantly remembered it as the text for the book Maurice and I had worked on. It had been misfiled and now it had resurfaced. She sent the manuscript to Michael di Capua, Maurice's and my longtime editor, and together they approached me about publishing it. We all agreed that, though the pictures were full-blown finished, the story needed some revision. Would I be willing to work on it? What a question!

With Maurice in my head and heart, remembering his voice, remembering our friendship, I took up my pencil. I refined the manuscript and here it is.

Forty-eight years ago, my friendship with Maurice took root over legendary Sutter's chocolate layer cake and the sweetness of our mutual loves—music, words, and pictures—now fused in this, our new collaboration. It was just meant to be.

ARTHUR YORINKS
January 2018